TELL ME ONE THING, DAD

Tom Pow

ILLUSTRATED BY

Ian Andrew

There are days like today
when Dad has read Molly
a story but she's not sleepy yet.

And she tucks up
all her cuddly toys
one by one,
then to begin their bedtime game
she asks, "Dad, tell me one thing –
the most important thing – you know
about a polar bear."

"About a polar bear?" Dad says.
"Yes, Dad, a polar bear."

"Now would that be the same
polar bear that lives on
the Arctic ice,

whose feet are the size of dinner plates,
whose teeth are
twice as bright;

the polar bear that swims
more elegantly
than it runs,

that shakes itself
like a car wash
and is dry as a bone
at once?"

"Yes, Dad,"
Molly says,
"that polar
bear."

"Well," he says, "I know that it loves its babies."

Molly nods her head. She's thinking, then she thinks some more, and, as she thinks,

Dad pretends that he's thinking even more.

"Dad, tell me one thing you know about a crocodile."

"About a croc-o-dile?" Dad says. "Yes, Dad, you know, the crocodile."

"A-ha, the crocodile," Dad says,
"the one that lies low
by the banks of the Nile,
whose skin is cracked
like dried-up mud,

whose teeth look like they're filed;
the crocodile that in the
blink of its yellow eye
rises from the stillest still
with a flash of its whip-crack tail

and a long, long, long, long smile?"

"Yes, Dad," Molly says,
"that's the crocodile."

"Well," he says,
"I know that it loves
its babies."

And again Molly nods
her head and gives a little clap
and she thinks some more, and,
as she thinks, Dad begins
to smile now – more and more.

"Dad, tell me, if you can,
one thing you know
about a dinosaur."

"Was that a dadosaur
you said?" Dad asks.

"No, Dad, a dinosaur."

"A-ha, the dinosaurs –

for indeed there were so many.
Some had necks like flumes
at the pool, some huge jaws that could
swallow a school; some skipped

on dancers' legs while clutching
invisible handbags; and one laid a single
egg that could've kept our street
for a week in omelettes!"

"Yes, Dad,"
Molly says,
"the dinosaurs."

"Well," Dad says,

then together they say – very loudly –
"We know that they loved their babies!"

M olly and Dad are both smiling
now, wide as crocodiles, and as
Molly thinks, Dad smiles
more and more –
but Molly,
she's smiling more
and more
AND MORE!

But the game's not over yet.

"Dad, tell me one thing you know"
(Molly says it oh so slowly)
"about a ... Grimalken."

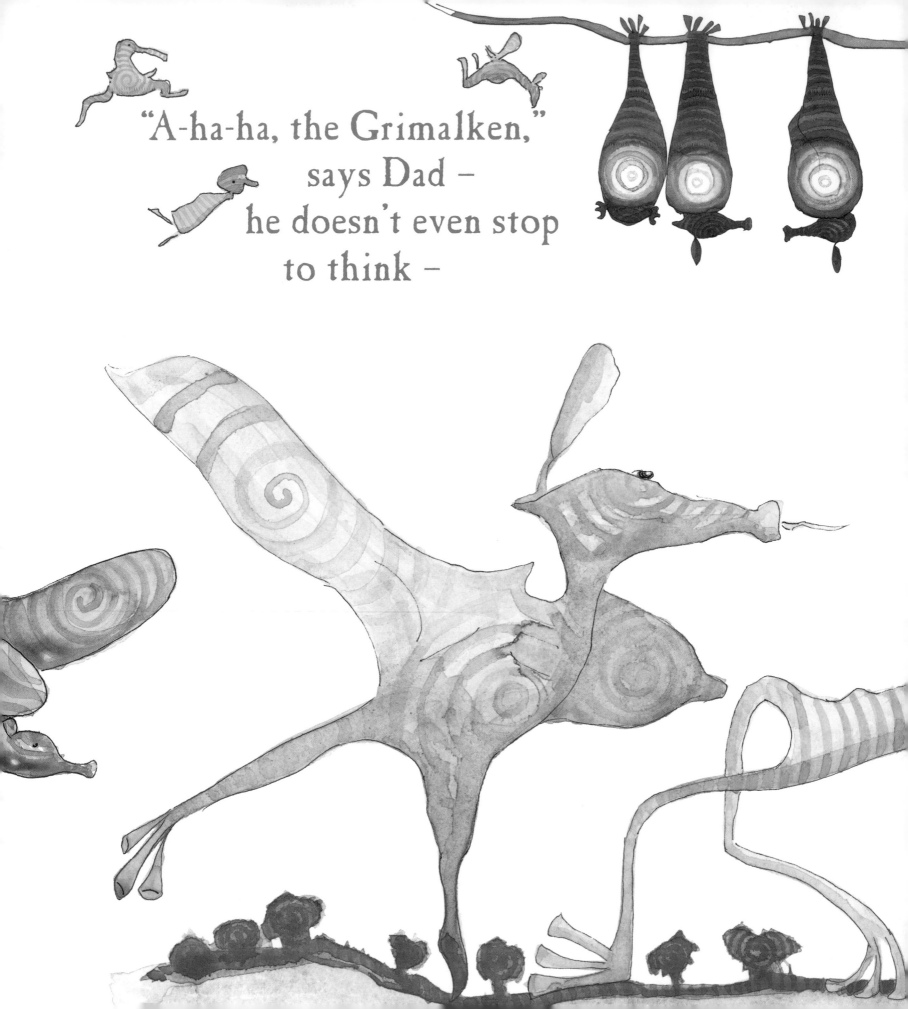

"A-ha-ha, the Grimalken,"
says Dad –
he doesn't even stop
to think –

"that'll be
the Grimalken that dances
on the green edge of town
and flinges with its
flooter at
night,

that grogs its kropotkins
all day long,

that flies
through the air
with its flanges intact,
that hoots
with its toes
when it snores..."

"Yes, Dad, all right,"
Molly says,
"that'll be the one."

"Well," he says,
"I know – and you do too! –
that it loves its
babies."

"**A**nd now
it's getting late," Dad says,
"so I want my turn now."

And he scratches his head
and thinks and thinks, and
as he thinks, Molly's
smiling more and more.
She can't help it!
"Come on, Dad," she says.

"OK," he says.
"Tell me, if you please,
one thing you know
about me."

"About you, Dad?"
says Molly.
"Mmmm, let me think..."

"I know you like
to disappear
with the paper
for hours and hours;

you keep your shoes
under the bed and pretend
your socks come up
smelling of
flowers;

the back of your neck is ticklish,
your fear of spiders is zilch
– my hero! –

and you
can throw me
so high in
the sky,

I won't come
back down till
tomorrow!"

"Yes," Dad says, "but what's the **most** important thing you know about me?"

"I think..."
Molly says.

"You're right!" Dad says.
"You know that
   I love my baby."